To Olive, Henry, and Megan

Additional color by Joan Wirolinggo

ISBN 978-0-06-300221-0
Library of Congress Control Number: 2020934465

Design by Joe Merkel
21 22 23 SCP 10 9 8 7 6 5 4 3 2
❖
First Edition

Trash Truck

Written and illustrated by
Max Keane

In a small town lived a big truck named Trash Truck . . .

and a little boy named Hank.

Hank and Trash Truck looked different,
but they were actually quite alike.

They both loved finding lost treasure . . .

and had a taste for adventure.

They didn't mind getting a little messy . . .

and both enjoyed
cleanup time.

They were even alike in what they disliked . . .

like accidents . . .

or having to be brave.

It's not always easy being a little kid in a big world . . .

or a big truck in a small town.

But then one day . . .

something amazing happened.

They found someone just like them. And together . . .

THE REAL HANK & Trash Truck

This is my son Henry, who showed our family how special trash trucks really are. One of the first words Henry said while looking out the car window at a garbage truck was "tra-tru-k!" From then on, that big truck that visited our house every Thursday had a name: Trash Truck. One night while putting Henry to bed, I told him a story about a little boy named Hank whose best friend was a big, kind-hearted garbage truck named—yep, you guessed it—Trash Truck! And now that bedtime story has become an animated series.

If you're a trash truck enthusiast like Henry or know someone who is, I hope you enjoy this story. And if you happen to be a trash truck reading this story, remember, you might just find that your new best friend is waiting at the window for you.

their world became just the right size.